This Little Tiger book belongs to:

_____

_____

_____

For Joshua David Constant
and Hannah Linda Constant,
with love ~ L C

For Noah ~ J C

LITTLE TIGER PRESS
1 The Coda Centre, 189 Munster Road, London SW6 6AW
www.littletigerpress.com
First published in Great Britain 2000
This edition published 2012
by Little Tiger Press, London
Text copyright © Linda Cornwell 2000
Illustrations copyright © Jane Chapman 2000
Linda Cornwell and Jane Chapman have asserted their rights
to be identified as the author and illustrator of this work
under the Copyright, Designs and Patents Act, 1988
All rights reserved • ISBN 978-1-85430-667-8
Printed in China • LTP/1900/0459/0512
2 4 6 8 10 9 7 5 3 1

Two Hungry Bears

Linda Cornwell and Jane Chapman

LITTLE TIGER PRESS

Big Brown Bear and Little Bear shared a den. They shared each other's company . . .

. . . and they shared
each other's food.
Little Bear nibbled
the edges . . .

and Big Brown Bear
munched up the middles.
In this way, they got
along very well.

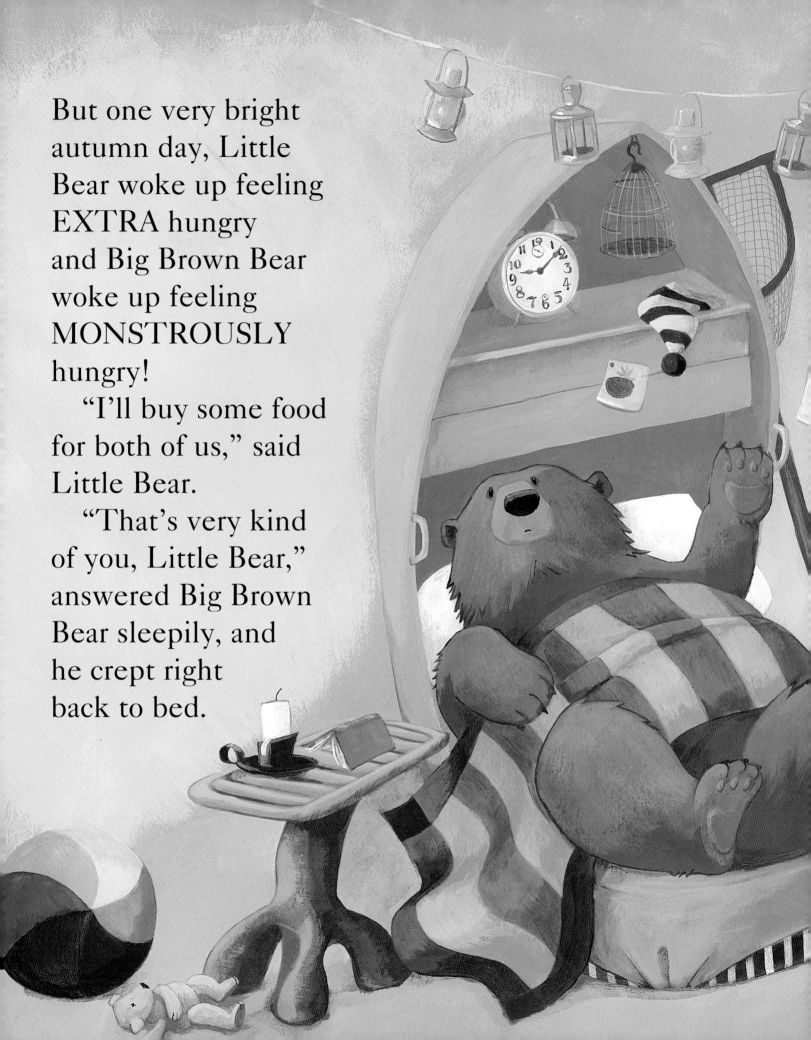

But one very bright autumn day, Little Bear woke up feeling EXTRA hungry and Big Brown Bear woke up feeling MONSTROUSLY hungry!

"I'll buy some food for both of us," said Little Bear.

"That's very kind of you, Little Bear," answered Big Brown Bear sleepily, and he crept right back to bed.

Little Bear went out
shopping and bought
some things to take
back to Big Brown
Bear. But she found
she was so hungry . . .

. . . that she ate everything
straight away –
pies and pastries
and peanuts,

chocolates and cheeses
and cakes . . .

from sides to middles,
middles to sides
AND BACK AGAIN!

Meanwhile, Big Brown Bear's tummy was
RRRRUMMMBLING so loudly
that the walls of the cave began to shake.
"I've been thinking," said Big Brown Bear,
"perhaps *I* should be out shopping for Little Bear."
So off he went with his big bag . . .

. . . but when he had filled
it right up, he was so
hungry that he found
he could not wait.

He began by
munching just
the middles.

But then he set to work on sausages,
strawberries and sandwiches,
not to mention tangerines and
toffee and tarts . . .

. . . AND
hamburgers
and custard . . .

AND
spaghetti
and soup . . .

AND
pizzas and salads . . .

AND
tomatoes and corn
and one small
grape.

Big Brown Bear ate tops, bottoms,
sides and middles.
There was just no stopping him!

But when he had finished eating,
he began to feel very, very full
and very, very guilty.
He had left nothing for Little Bear.

Big Brown Bear staggered back home where
Little Bear was waiting patiently for him.
   "Did you find any nice middles to munch?"
Little Bear asked him.
   "*I can see that you did!*" she thought to herself.
   Big Brown Bear could only nod his head.

   "Did you come across any tasty edges to nibble?"
asked Big Brown Bear.
   "*It certainly looks as though you might have!*"
he thought to himself.

Then they sat
down together.
"I saved you half
of a cracker,"
said Big Brown Bear.
"It still has four
edges to nibble."
"I saved you three
quarters of a banana,"
said Little Bear.
"It's all middle, with
no edges
at all!"

After a while, Big
Brown Bear yawned.
"I think I'll skip supper,"
he said. "I'm feeling
a little too tired."
"An early night will
do us both good,"
agreed Little Bear.
They spent a very
long time brushing
their teeth . . .

before Big Brown Bear snuggled into his
bed, and Little Bear crept quietly into hers.

"Let's collect the food together tomorrow,"
yawned Big Brown Bear.

But tomorrow was a long, long time away
because . . .

. . . Big Brown Bear and
Little Bear slept, with
their tummies nicely full,
all through the winter until
SPRING!

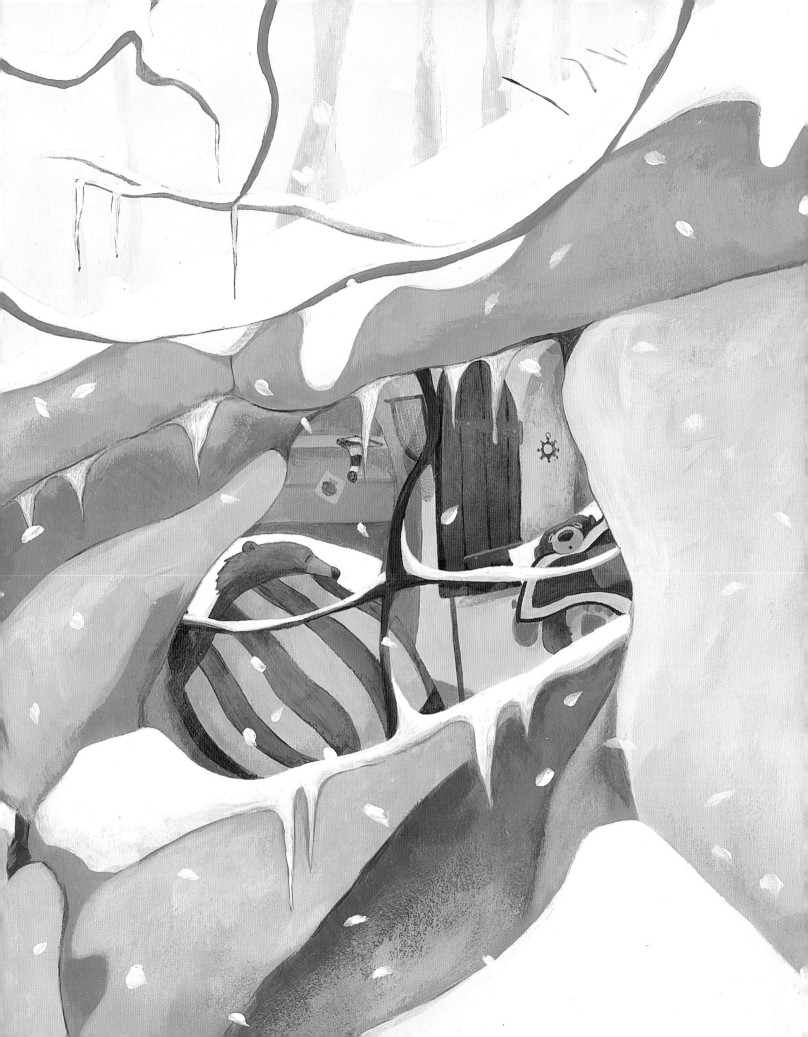